TOP SHELF PRODUCTIONS
MARIETTA, GA

ISBN 978-1-60309-349-1
Published by Top Shelf Productions, PO Box 1282, Marietta, GA 30061-1282, USA. Publishers: Brett Warnock and Chris Staros. Top Shelf Productions® and the Top Shelf logo are registered trademarks of Top Shelf Productions, Inc.
Visit our online catalog at www.topshelfcomix.com.

First Printing, September, 2014. Printed in China.

CHAPTER ONE:

ARE you Ready to ZOOM to the MOON on your skateboard, Johnny Boo?
I'm Ready, Squiggle.

Then brace yourself! This is going to be AMAZING!
Straight to the MOON!
3... 2... 1...

ZOOM!

Ha ha!
ZOOM ZOOM ZOOM!
ARE you having FUN, JohNNY Boo?

OR is it too SCARY fast? Should I zoom slower, JohNNy Boo?

Actually, we're NOT Really ZOOMING that fast at all, Squiggle.
We're kinda just zooming perfectly STILL.
Oh!

.K. ohnny Boo.

That might actually WORK! Good idea!

OOM

RAR!

SQUIGGLE SWISH

Huff huff huff.

I can do it!

RA

Squig
NEVE
give up

Keep pulling, Squiggle!
I can a
taste t
Moon Ic
alread

Roll
Roll
Roll

CHAPTER TWO:

Hey... isn't that Johnny Boo?
I think so.
Z
What's he doing?
Z

Z

It looks like he's riding a skateboard.
Cool.

I've never seen anyone ride so SLOWLY.
Yeah! Check it OUT!

Johnny Boo is an AWESOME Skateboarder.
I bet he knows a million cool tricks like that.

Z
Actually... I think he's asleep.

What? That's a silly skateboard trick.
Let's wake him up!
I'll tickle his foot.

Hello?! Are we there yet?
Tee hee

Is this the moon?
No, Johnny Boo.
It's a SKATEBOARD!

Oh.
You were doing a sleepy skateboard trick–
–so we woke you up!

YAWN
Hey!
NO YAWNING!

Night is no time to be a silly SLEEPYHEAD!
It's time to PLAY with us, Johnny Boo!

Sorry, guys.
I guess I fell asleep riding my skateboard to the MOON.

But you'll NEVER get there with those silly CIRCLE wheels.
I won't?
No WAY, Johnny Boo.
Z

What shape should I use? SQUARE?
No!
Triangle?
No!

Octodecapolyhexa-whatchamacallitagon?

No, Johnny Boo.
To go to the moon-
-you need STAR shaped wheels!
HOORAY!
Oh!
That almost makes sense.
Z Z Z

CHAPTER THREE:

We better count ourselves first, just to be sure.
Okay!

One.
Two!
Three!
Doggy!

Doggy is not a number!
Maybe it is.

How many legs does a doggy have?
Eleven?
FOUR!

Okay. So I guess there ARE four of us.
Goody!
That means we're READY!

We're ready to help now, Johnny Boo. Hold up your skateboard.

Like this?
Hold it tight! HeRe we come!

Attack!
ZIP ZIP ZIP ZIP ZIP
DING
DING
DING
DING

Hey! I think you guys kind of BROKE my skateboaRd. You bRoke the wheels off!
No way. We didn't bReak it, Johnny Boo.
We fixed it!
HooRay foR us!
HooRay foR STAR WHEELS!

I don't know about this, guys... aren't wheels round for a reason?
Nope.
Nuh-uh.
No reason.
None that I know of.

No... I'm pretty sure that round wheels roll better.
That's not true!
Stars are the coolest.

Fine.
I'll just show you. Promise you won't get all disappointedy and cry-ish.
We promise, Johnny Boo!

Well...
See what I mean? We're not rolling, are we?
I told you so.
Z

But... it would be cool if you were right.
Too bad.
Tee hee.
Tee hee.
Hee hee.

You haven't shouted "Skateboard Go" yet, Johnny Boo.
Skateboard go?

Come on, Johnny Boo!
You can shout LOUDER than that.
I thought you were "the best little ghost in the world".
Z Z Z

I am.
Well, prove it, Johnny Boo!

Oh, fine.
SKATEBOARD-

-GO!
Yipe!!!
WOOOSH
Ha ha!
Tee hee!
To the MOON, JOHNNY Boo!
Ho ho!
Z

CHAPTER FOUR:

Well,
Johnny Boo...
if you're SO
bored, maybe
you should try
doing some
cool
Skateboard
tricks!
Yeah!
Do a trick!

Okay, watch this.
I'll do a super one-footy.

Ta-da!
Boring.
Not cool enough.

Well... what SHOULD I do? An electric wiggle worm? A Boston Baked Bouncing Bean? A tubular toothpaste tumble-butt?

A front-row slider with a tornado twister backwards upsideways-down nuclear elbow felbow welbow shmelbow?

Yes! Do that one! The elbow felbow whatever!

Oh, I'll do one EVEN BETTER.
Check THIS out!

FRONT-NOSE slippy hurricane-spinner backwoods side-upwise-downish uncle kneecap blister twister mister ELBOW!
Wow!

BOOM!

Tee hee.
That was FUN, Johnny Boo.
Do it again!
Again!
ZZZ
Do WHAT again?

CHAPTER FIVE:

Where AM I?
You're on the MOON, Johnny Boo!

Who am I?

You're Johnny Boo, Johnny Boo!

What just happened? Why am I all dizzy?
You just did an awesome skateboard trick, Johnny Boo.
Z

Of course I did. But what happened after THAT?
Nothing.
I don't know.
I'm hungry!
I'm Charlie. Hi!

No... Something happened. I remember a BOOM.
Maybe you played the drums.
Maybe you tootered.
I happened, Johnny Boo.
Huh? Who are YOU?

I'm Susie Boom!
Hi Susie!
Oh!
A girl!

And I'm really mad at you, Johnny Boo.
What? Why?!
Just kidding!
Tricked you.

Also, I was the one who went BOOM.
Cool.
That was awesome.

Yeah. I'm the awesomest girl-ghost on the moon.

That's why they call me Susie Boom! HOORAY!
Well, that's a pretty good reason, I guess.
I know. Hooray!
Okay.
Hooray!
Hooray!
Hooray!

Okay.
HooRay!

Okay.
HooRay!

Okay, Susie Boom.
HooRay!

I said "okay."
HooRay!

Okayokayokay OKAY!
Enough with the hoorays!

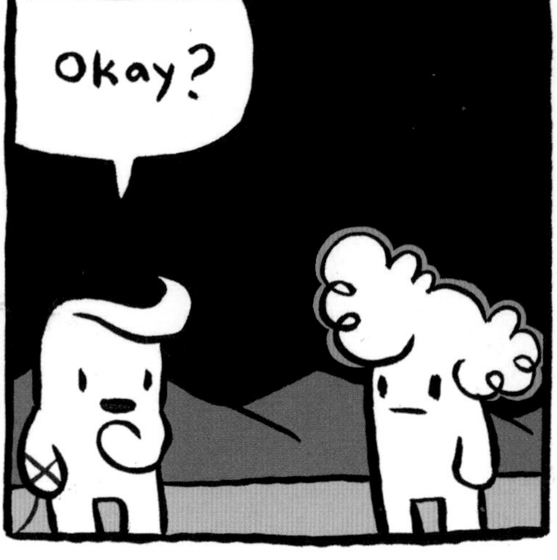
Okay?

But today is HOORAY DAY on the moon!
HOORAY!!
HOORAY!
Oookay.

CHAPTER SIX:

Hey! I KNOW what this party Needs!
MOON ICE CREAM!
Oh!
DON'T say that, JOHNNY Boo!

Why? Where is all the ice cream, anyways? I thought the moon was FULL of it.

AND...
Come to think of it... where are all the stars?

What are WE, Johnny Boo? Chopped liver?
I mean all the other stars.

So, what's up, Susie Boom? Where are all the STARS and ICE CREAM?
DON'T SAY that!

Don't say what? Stars?
Shh!

Ice cream?
Johnny Boo! No!!

What? Did I accidentally say a secret moon swear, or-
Did Someone SAY ICE CREAM?
Oh no! It's HIM!

HOORAY!
AN ICE CREAM MONSTER!

EEK!
SNATCH!
Johnny Boo!

Z
PLOP
More ice cream for my giant HOORAY DAY cone!
Ha ha HOORAY!

And more TWINKLE SPRINKLE STARS!
Hey.
What?!
No!

Eek!
CATCH!

We're not sprinkles!
YES YOU ARE!

Nooo!
PLOP
SPRINKLE SPRINKLE!

Happy HOORAY DAY!!!
Help!
Help!
Help!
Help!
ZZZ
Ha HO!
Johnny Boo!
Are you okay?

Mmf mmf mmf!!
I can't Boo!

Don't WORRY, Johnny Boo. I'll SAVE you.

Because I'm Susie-
BOOM

CHAPTER SEVEN:

Z

Yawn!
Hmmm. It's morning.
Wake up, Johnny Boo!
GOOD MORNING! ♫
Huh?
What?
Oh!
Susie!!
Silly Johnny Boo!
My name isn't SUSIE!

No, Squiggle! I just met the coolest girl!
You did?
Her name is Susie Boom and she lives on the MOON!
Oh, silly Johnny Boo. You must have been only DREAMING!
We never made it to the Moon. We fell asleep trying, remember?
Well, yeah... but...

I Really did go to the Moon!
After we fell asleep. I woke back up and...
and...
and...

And now you have an imaginary GIRLFRIEND!
Tee hee!

Hey. I didn't say she was my GIRLFRIEND.
Ha ha!
I just said that she was REALLY COOL.

Hmmph.
I'm SORRY, Johnny Boo.
I didn't mean to tease you.

But everyone knows the MOON isn't real.
It's just a funny light in the sky. You can't really GO there.
So of course you-
BOOM
Uh-oh. I hear thunder, Johnny Boo. I think it's going to rain.
That's not THUNDER, Squiggle.

That's Susie Boom!
Happy Hooray Day, boys!
I brought MOON ICE CREAM to share!
Oh!
HOORay!

THE END!

A PHOTO OF
THE AUTHOR AT WORK: